Jack's Basket

for Jack, Emma and Jamie

A Red Fox Book

Published by Random House Children's Books
20 Vauxhall Bridge Road, London SW1V 2SA

A division of The Random House Group Ltd
London Melbourne Sydney Auckland
Johannesburg and agencies throughout the world

1 3 5 7 9 10 8 6 4 2

First published in Great Britain by
Hutchinson Children's Books 1987
Red Fox edition 2000

Printed in Singapore by Tien Wah Press (PTE) Ltd

THE RANDOM HOUSE GROUP Limited Reg. No. 954009

www.randomhouse.co.uk

ISBN 0 09 940945 3

ALISON CATLEY
Jack's Basket

When Baby Jack came home from the hospital, his sister Kate didn't think he was much to look at. He was so tiny, so red and wrinkled. And so squally.

Jack was too small for a crib. So
they got him a straw basket instead.

He slept in it night and day
until he grew too big.

Kate gave Jack her old crib, and the cats took over the basket. They played in it and crawled all over it. So did Jack.

When Jack was two, the basket made
a perfect racing car for him. With a
broom for a mast, it made a fine ship.

It could hold a picnic lunch
to take to the beach,

or the laundry when the children
had to help Mother.

Each fall, Jack and Kate filled the basket with apples to take home.

Jack turned six. By then there were holes in the sides of the basket. The handles were torn, and it wasn't much use anymore.

So it was thrown in a corner of the
shed, where it lay through the seasons,
forgotten by the family.

A field mouse discovered the basket,

and it was still a fine place for babies
to sleep.